Puppy Mudge Takes a Bath

Puppy Mudge Takes a Bath

By Cynthia Rylant

Illustrated by Isidre Mones

in the style of Suçie Stevenson

SCHOLASTIC INC.
New York Toronto London Auckland Sydney
Mexico City New Delhi Hong Kong Buenos Aires

ISBN 0-439-56134-5

Text copyright © 2002 by Cynthia Rylant.
Illustrations copyright © 2002 by Suçie Stevenson.
All rights reserved.
Published by Scholastic Inc., 557 Broadway, New York, NY 10012,
by arrangement with Simon & Schuster Books for Young Readers,
Simon & Schuster Children's Publishing Division.
SCHOLASTIC and associated logos are trademarks
and/or registered trademarks of Scholastic Inc.

12 11 10 9 8 7 6 5 4 3 2 1   3 4 5 6 7 8/0

Printed in the U.S.A.   23

First Scholastic printing, September 2003

Book design by Mark Siegel
The text of this book is set in Goudy.

This is Henry.

This is Henry's puppy Mudge.
Mudge loves mud.

Mud makes Mudge roll.

And roll.
And roll.

Mudge is muddy.
Mudge needs a bath.

There is the tub.

Where is Mudge?

Mudge is hiding.
Mudge does not love tubs.

Henry finds Mudge.

Mudge is in the tub.

Now Henry is in the tub!
Mudge is happy.

Mudge is very clean.
Henry is very clean.

The tub is very muddy!

Henry and Mudge dry off.
They go back outside.

Look what Mudge found.

Mudge is smelly.

Mudge needs a bath.

There is the tub.

Where is Mudge?

Here we go again.